The Hungry Little Gator

By Alexis Braud

Illustrated by Allison Dugas Behan

PELICAN PUBLISHING
New Orleans 2021

Copyright © 2020
By Alexis Braud

Illustrations copyright © 2020
By Allison Dugas Behan
All rights reserved

First River Road Press printing, 2020
First Pelican Publishing printing, 2021

ISBN 9781455626847
Ebook ISBN 9781455626854

The word "Pelican" and the depiction of a pelican are trademarks of Arcadia Publishing Company Inc. and are registered in the U.S. Patent and Trademark Office

Printed in Korea
Published by Pelican Publishing
New Orleans, LA
www.pelicanpub.com

The Hungry Little Gator likes to eat!

The Hungry Little Gator likes Louisiana treats.

How many treats can that little Gator eat?

ONE sloppy po' boy measured in feet.

TWO dozen tamales bought on the street.

3 THREE trays of oysters on ice can't compete.

4 FOUR fat pralines
so salty and sweet.

FIVE bowls of gumbo, each quite unique.

6 SIX fried balls of something that's probably meat.

SEVEN beignets with coffee—
no way to be neat.

EIGHT dozen crawfish with corn and potatoes! Tout suite!

9 NINE seafood platters, each a tall, deep-fried feat.

10 TEN brightly colored sno-balls, and the day is complete!